1 8 MAY 2022

Hw

Richmond upon Thames Libraries

Renew online at www.richmond.gov.uk/libraries

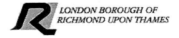

LONDON BOROUGH OF
RICHMOND UPON THAMES

'Merkid Rescue'
An original concept by Elizabeth Dale
© Elizabeth Dale 2022

Illustrated by Giorgia Broseghini

Published by MAVERICK ARTS PUBLISHING LTD
Studio 11, City Business Centre, 6 Brighton Road,
Horsham, West Sussex, RH13 5BB
© Maverick Arts Publishing Limited February 2022
+44 (0)1403 256941

A CIP catalogue record for this book is available at the British Library.

ISBN 978-1-84886-861-8

www.maverickbooks.co.uk

This book is rated as: White Band (Guided Reading)

Merkid Rescue

by Elizabeth Dale

illustrated by
Giorgia Broseghini

Chapter 1

Alex was having the best time. He had come with his mum and sister, Mary, to the beach. The sun was shining, the sea sparkled blue and the smell of sun cream was everywhere. He cheered as Mary planted a flag on top of the huge sandcastle they'd just built.

"Can we go in the sea now?" he asked his mum.

"Okay," she said, smiling.

"Hooray!" cried Mary. "I just need to blow up Magica!"

Alex grinned. He'd given Mary a unicorn floaty for her birthday and she absolutely loved it. She called it Magica because she said all unicorns were magic. She puffed air into the ring as fast as she could, but it came back out again almost as quickly!

"Here, let me help," Alex said, and Mary handed Magica over.

"Right," said their mum when he'd finished. "Let's go! But we must only go in the sea between those red and yellow flags where the lifeguards are watching. That's the only safe place to swim."

Mary jumped up. "Oh... I need to go to the toilet!" she said.

Alex sighed. How typical of Mary! Just when they were about to do something fun, she always needed to go to the toilet. "Can't you wait?" he asked.

"Alex, be patient," said their mum. "We'll only be five minutes. You stay here and look after our things, then we'll have lots of time in the sea when we get back."

"Okay…" Alex said. As Mum and Mary went to the toilets, he started digging a road from their castle. There was a sudden gust of wind and something blew past him, bashing his ear.
Oh no, it was Magica! And it was being blown into the sea!

Chapter 2

Alex jumped up and chased after the floaty as fast as he could. Another gust blew Magica. There was nobody nearby to grab it, so Alex splashed in after it. A wave brought Magica closer and then took it away again. Alex waded into the water, deeper and deeper, and then a wave brought Magica back again.
Alex jumped forward and grabbed it. He'd got it!

But when Alex tried to wade back to the beach,
his feet couldn't touch the ground. The water
was too deep. He jumped up onto Magica and
lay across it to paddle into calmer water before
heading back to shore. This was fun!

Suddenly, Alex saw his mum rushing to the sea's edge. Oh no! She looked really upset. And no wonder! He'd gone far out into the sea on his own, and he wasn't between the flags where the lifeguards patrolled. But it wasn't his fault. He'd better get back quick and explain.

Alex paddled as fast as he could, but somehow he didn't get any closer to the shore. In fact he seemed to be going further away! He started to panic.

"Oi!"

When he heard the shout, Alex turned. He could see a boy and girl swimming towards him from further out. They were waving and yelling.

Alex waved back.

"You need to turn and head that way!" cried the boy, pointing across the bay. "You're caught in a dangerous riptide*. It might look calm where you are, but there is a strong current under the water."

Really? But the way they wanted him to go was really choppy. But Alex had to stop being pulled out to sea so he quickly started paddling hard in the direction the boy had pointed, but he wasn't actually going that way at all. Instead, the current was still pulling him away from the beach.

"I can't do it!" he yelled desperately. "Help!"

A riptide is a strong current that can pull anything in it out to sea. It is a narrow band of smooth-looking water with choppy water either side.

Chapter 3

Alex paddled harder than ever, but the strong current carried him even further out. He looked back to shore. His mum and Mary were running over to the lifeguard post, waving madly. Thank goodness they'd seen the problem. But would the lifeguards be able to rescue him before he was swept far out to sea?

And then Alex saw the boy and girl again. Instead of swimming to safety, they were heading through the rough sea towards him.

They were swimming into the riptide!

"Hold on!" the girl cried. "We'll save you!"

Alex couldn't believe his luck! He watched as
the two children swam into the smooth riptide
water. Then they both grabbed hold of Magica
and started pushing it as they swam. Slowly but
surely, Alex was moving across the bay.

Finally, they reached the choppy water but at least the current was no longer pulling them out to sea. They were out of the riptide! Hooray!

"Thank you," Alex said to the boy and girl. "You saved my life! Who are you?"

"I'm Jessie and this is my brother, Max," said the girl.

"Are you champion swimmers or something?" asked Alex.

Max laughed. "No, of course not."

"Well you were brilliant to save me," said Alex. "How can I ever repay you?"

Max looked at Jessie. "There is one thing we really want you to do," he said.

"What?" asked Alex. "I'll do anything."

"Don't tell anyone about us," said Jessie.

"What?" asked Alex. "But you deserve medals! I have to tell everyone!"

"No," said Jessie, "you mustn't. We've broken our code to help you today. We aren't allowed to let humans see us. But we had to save you."

Alex frowned. "I don't understand. What code?"

"The mercode!" said Max.

And with a swish he lifted his long, shimmering, green tail out of the sea and splashed it back down into the water.

Alex was so startled that he fell off Magica!

SPLASH!

Chapter 4

And so, Max and Jessie had to rescue Alex all over again. They dived down and pulled him, spluttering, to the surface.

"Climb up onto your unicorn," said Jessie.

Alex did as she said and then he lay there, gasping for breath, staring at Max and Jessie.

"You're... you're mermaids!" he cried.

"I'm not!" said Max indignantly. "I'm not a girl. Jessie's a mermaid, I'm a merboy."

"A merboy?" said Alex. "Sorry. I didn't even know they existed. Well, I didn't know mermaids really existed either," he said. "I mean, I've read about them. But I've never heard of anyone who's actually seen them."

"That's because we're not allowed to show ourselves to humans," said Max. "All merkids are told that from birth."

"So we've been keeping behind you so no one can see us from the shore. You mustn't tell anyone about us," said Jessie. "Please!"

"Okay," said Alex.

"Look, the lifeguard's coming to help you," said Max. "We have to go."

"Stay safe!" called Jessie.

"I will," said Alex. "Thank you so much."
He watched the merkids dive down deep into
the sea. Then he paddled to meet the lifeguard,

who was swimming towards him pulling a rescue tube.

"Are you okay?" he yelled.

"Yes, thank you," said Alex.

"Here, climb onto the tube," said the lifeguard. "You'll be safer on that than the floaty unicorn."

Alex did as he was told, tightly clasping Magica.

There was no way he was

letting go of it now!

As the lifeguard quickly towed Alex back to the beach, a crowd gathered. His mum and Mary rushed forward to meet him and Alex braced himself for a huge telling-off from his mum. But instead, she and Mary hugged him.

"You're safe!" his mum cried. "Thank goodness. I thought we'd lost you!"

"No," Alex smiled. "I'm sorry, Mum. Magica blew into the sea, I had to catch it for Mary. But I got caught in the riptide."

"That's why we have the flags to show you where it's safe to swim," said the lifeguard. "The water in the riptide is much smoother than the waves either side of it, fooling swimmers that it's safe. But it's a very strong current that drags swimmers out to sea. I'm amazed you managed to paddle out of it."

"Oh, it wasn't just me, it was m..." Alex stopped. He'd nearly given away the merkids' secret!

"Magica helped you, didn't he?" said Mary. "You rescued him and then you rode on him and he saved you."

"Er, yes..." said Alex.

Mary took her floaty from Alex and hugged it. "Thank you so much for rescuing Magica. I'm sorry, I'll never ask to go to the toilet again!"

Alex laughed. "Don't worry about that! It wasn't your fault, I'll be more careful in the future."

"Please do," his mum said as she gave Alex, Mary and Magica a big hug. "You were very lucky just now."

Alex smiled. He was far luckier than she knew!

As they settled down to eat their picnic, Alex thought about everything that had happened.

He would never ever forget today, meeting the merkids and his incredibly amazing merkid rescue.

The End

Book Bands for Guided Reading

The Institute of Education book banding system is a scale of colours that reflects the various levels of reading difficulty. The bands are assigned by taking into account the content, the language style, the layout and phonics. Word, phrase and sentence level work is also taken into consideration.

Maverick Early Readers are a bright, attractive range of books covering the pink to white bands. All of these books have been book banded for guided reading to the industry standard and edited by a leading educational consultant.

Pink

Red

Yellow

Blue

Green

Orange

Turquoise

Purple

Gold

White

To view the whole Maverick Readers scheme, visit our website at www.maverickearlyreaders.com

Or scan the QR code above to view our scheme instantly!